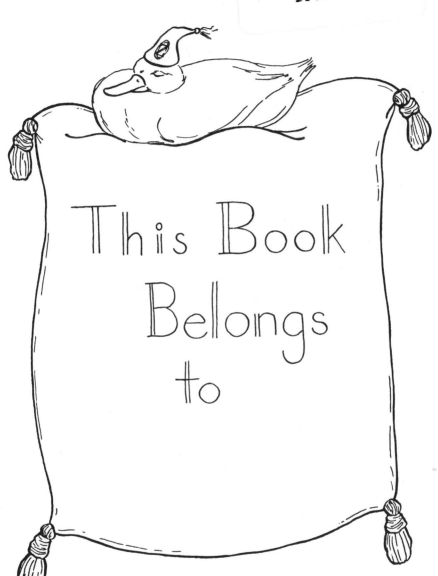

This Book

Belongs

to

The Lavender Bear of Oz

THE
LAVENDER BEAR
OF OZ

Written and Illustrated

By

Bill Campbell
and
Irwin Terry

NEW YORK

The Emerald City Press

1998

The Lavender Bear of Oz

Printed in the U.S.A.

The Emerald City Press
A Division Of
Books of Wonder
16 West 18th Street, New York, NY 10011

ISBN 0-929605-77-2 (paperback)

ISBN 0-929605-83-7 (limited edition)

1 2 3 4 5 6 7 8 9

Dedicated to:

Big Teddy

Dom Dom's Cousin

Teddy Edward

And All The Other Bears...

List of Chapters

Bear Center

The sun was just sinking toward the horizon when a small white duck flew into the Winkie Country of the marvelous land of Oz. "Hmm. Very yellow," he thought as he looked at the ground below. "I wonder if those large trees are laburnums?" Flying lower to get a closer look, the duck's tail feathers brushed the tops of the tall trees. He was in the middle of a forest, at the edge of a clearing next to a river. Deciding to take a rest, the duck flew down and landed with a skid in the yellow grass that was dotted with buttercups.

Standing on his webbed feet and flapping his wings to smooth his feathers, the white duck rested in the clearing and looked around. The trees surrounding the grassy spot were indeed huge old laburnum trees which were in full bloom with their bright yellow flowers hanging in picturesque ringlets, circling the vivid blue patch of sky in a blaze of gold.

Waddling around the clearing, snapping at daffodils, the duck came upon a large puddle in which he could see his reflection. "Oh my! This

1

will never do!" he clucked, as he saw a streak of yellow from the grass staining his bright white feathers. Hopping into the puddle, the duck splashed and spluttered, quacking happily while cleaning himself in the warm evening sunshine. Ducking his head below the surface of the water, he found some delicious golden squosh to eat, and feasted merrily. When he had finished, he looked up in surprise to find himself surrounded by bears of every size and color.

"Goodness!" squawked the duck, looking this way and that to see if there were room for an emergency take-off.

"What is it?" asked a small green bear as she tugged at the arm of the Blue Bear standing next to her.

"Hush now," replied the Blue Bear with a snort. "We ought to inform the King that something has gotten past the sentry."

The duck paddled around the small puddle, examining the bears, and came to a stop in front of the Blue Bear. Waddling out of the puddle, the duck shook out his feathers, drenching the bear with a spray of water, and gave an insulted quack. "I am not a *something* thank you very much. I am a duck."

"What did he say?" asked an elderly grey bear at the opposite end of the puddle.

"I said DUCK!" shouted the duck at the Grey Bear. At once all the bears in the clearing fell flat on their faces with their arms over their heads. The duck looked around in amusement and, with a flap of his wings, perched himself on a large rock in the center of the glade.

As the bewildered bears began to stand and brush the grass from their knees, the Blue Bear trotted over to the duck and looked at him disapprovingly. "Just who are you and what do you want?" he demanded, raising himself to his full height (which wasn't very tall at all).

The duck, who had been looking intently at the bears, ignored the question. "What kind of bears are you anyway?" he asked in a sarcastic tone.

"We're very proper sorts of bears. This is the glorious city of Bear Center, and we're the most bear-like bears you'll find anywhere."

"Proper sort of bears indeed!" huffed the duck. "I've been all the world over and I wouldn't call you proper bears. Look at you! You're sewn together with jointed arms and legs, and you appear to be stuffed with fluff."

"Fluff!! I'll have you know that we are stuffed with only the nicest curled hair and our skin is the finest plush," replied the Blue Bear in a petulant tone.

This was true, for the bears were all made from the best materials, and their heads, arms and legs were jointed in a superior manner. As for their costumes, some were decked out in a variety of colorful hats, while others had brocade vests or waistcoats. Baggy pantaloons seemed to be a popular fashion, as were large lace collars and ribbons of all sorts. Each bear was fitted out with a toy weapon or noise-maker to use while on sentry duty, for the bears of Bear Center each took turns guarding the city from intruders. Due to their vigilance, the bears resided quite peacefully in the clearing, spending their days playing games or tending to the trees. Each bear lived in a hollow in one of the laburnum trees that surrounded the glade, and the king of this small enclave lived high above the others in an elaborate tree-house in the tallest tree.

Getting back to the business at hand, the Blue Bear harumphed and then, addressing the duck, ordered, "State your name and business."

"My name is Seymour."

The Grey Bear snickered loudly and hid his smile with his paw.

Highly offended, the duck glowered at the laughing bear. "As I have already stated, I travel a great deal and see more than the average duck. That is why my name is Seymour. As for my business, I have no business with you. I just happened to be flying past, noticed the lovely trees in this clearing and thought I'd take a short rest."

"He's probably here to spy on us," whispered an olive bear to the Blue Bear.

An excitable crimson bear piped up, "He's in league with the squirrels!"

Nodding in agreement, the Blue Bear motioned for the other bears to surround the rock, ordering that Seymour be taken to the King. The duck, who was getting more annoyed by the minute, hopped down from the rock and waddled straight up to the Blue Bear. Tilting his head to one side, Seymour grinned wickedly and loudly quacked, "A proper bear indeed! I'll bet you have a squeaker in your chest."

A gasp rose from the crowd. Personal remarks concerning the noisemakers built into the various bears were considered to be in the poorest taste. Aghast, the Blue Bear stepped back a pace and replied, "I'll have you know that I have a double action growler!" Doing a cartwheel and stopping when he was upside down, a rather impressive growl emanated from the Blue Bear's chest. As he righted himself, his chest growled again. A smattering of applause filled the air, and the Blue Bear proudly bowed left and right. Unfortunately, he then tripped over a tree root and landed smack on top of the duck. Seymour squawked and tumbled backwards, hitting a toy gun which let out a tremendous BANG!

The unexpected noise so startled the bears that they quickly vanished into their trees. All, that is, except the Blue Bear, who picked himself up and grabbed hold of the duck's wing, ushering him in the direction of the King's tree. As he pulled the unwilling duck along he grumbled, "I think it's time we visited the King. He'll find out just what you're up to."

In Merryland

"If I see one more bottle of milk, I'll scream so loud it will straighten their curly wool!" the King of the Babies vowed to himself. Minutes later a large bottle of creamy milk arrived, right on schedule, and that was the day the King of the Babies decided to revolt.

Now you must understand that this particular baby wasn't really the *king* of the babies, for the babies of Babyland have no infant ruler. This baby, just one of many infants, lived on a pink cloud over a lovely valley which was part of a larger country called Merryland, which lies to the east of the land of Oz. Merryland is a charming country, consisting of seven pretty valleys, each one filled with different sorts of happy and unusual inhabitants. The babies reside in and above Merryland's third valley, which is particularly soothing and pleasant with delicate perfumes and floating lullabies filling the air.

8

In Merryland

Near a large milk fountain at the center of this valley, storks prepare the many infants who will be delivered to expectant families in the outside world. The storks must keep busy with their deliveries because of the steady stream of new babies that arrive in the valley in a rather unusual way. High above the valley floats the large pink cloud, and it is on this cloud that babies are prepared. When happy and healthy, each new infant is wrapped in a soft pink baby blossom and dropped down through the sky to the Merryland valley.

Life begins for each baby on the cloud in a peaceful and tranquil way. The guardians of the infants are fluffy pink sheep, who closely watch over the babies, feeding them and caring for their every need. The babies are gently rocked in their prams and coddled, and at the end of each day the sheep delight in leaping over fences to coax the infants to sleep. Once the babies are snuggled in their beds, the sheep spend the twilight hours carding and spinning their wool, which they then use to knit cozy caps, baby booties and blankets for their charges. All in all, life for both babies and sheep is peaceful and quiet—however just at present a crisis was occurring.

Having decided upon a revolt, the King of the Babies was quick to act. Many babies can be crabby, but this was obviously the biggest baby in Babyland. As is often the case, the King of the Babies was also the cutest, most picture-perfect baby imaginable — when asleep. When awake, he could hold his breath until he was bright blue in the face, yell louder, burp-up further, and make himself into the crankiest baby one would ever hope to see. The sheep were used to the baby's tantrums, which occurred on a daily basis, but they did not realize that for some time this particular baby was making plans.

He had already stolen the biggest blanket for his royal robe, and had secretly commandeered a spyglass from the supply cupboard. He had planned a full-scale baby revolt against the sheep, and he did all of this because something was missing. He wasn't quite sure *what* was missing, but he knew there had to be more to life than caps, booties and regular naps. Being of an adventurous nature, he decided to go and find what else there might be.

Convincing the other babies to follow his plans was fairly simple. He merely pointed out that none of the babies who were sent floating from the

cloud were ever seen again. This aroused the suspicions of the simple infants, and the revolt was promptly organized. Utilizing their prams, which were very co-operative vehicles, the babies constructed a sturdy fortress in the middle of the blossom field. As the sheep, who were naturally concerned for the well-being of their charges, tried to cajole and cheer the infants, they found themselves corralled and captured.

In the valley below, the storks were concerned that production was coming to a standstill, due to an unusually long period of time in which no new babies had arrived from the sky. A meeting was held, and the storks decided that a delegation should fly up and find out what was causing the interruption, when all at once blossoms began to arrive at a breakneck pace. As they gently touched the ground and spread their petals, the storks were horrified to see that each blossom bore not a baby, but a pink sheep which had been cleverly bound with fluffy yarn so it couldn't move, and gagged with a diaper and a pacifier tucked in its mouth. In alarm, several storks were dispatched to fly up to the pink cloud.

Peering over the edge of the cloud with his spyglass, the King of the Babies spotted the storks flapping their way in his direction. Using a stale piece of arrowroot biscuit, he sliced through the wispy tethers that held the pink cloud in place above Merryland. To their dismay, the approaching storks saw the cloud of babies swiftly sail away on the wind, while the remaining pink sheep gently sailed to the valley below on a cluster of blossoms.

The Lavender Bear

The Blue Bear led Seymour to a tall tree at the opposite edge of the clearing. "Our king is above us all in this fine tree," he stated proudly. "He lives here in his castle with the Little Pink Bear, who acts as his advisor. We're very proud of them both."

The duck gave an exasperated snort, then resigned himself to being pushed and prodded up the tree by the Blue Bear. "You do realize I could just fly up here, don't you?" he snapped. "Ducks are not made for climbing."

With a grunt for a reply, the Blue Bear continued pushing until the odd pair finally reached a platform halfway up the tree. Here there was a stair that continued, spiraling up the trunk to a leafy castle which was woven from the growing branches of the tree. Soft light filtered through the leaves and laburnum blossoms, and clever twisting and braiding of the soft branches

14

created lovely patterns in the walls. "Not bad," sniffed Seymour, who had never seen anything so marvelous in his life. "A bit rustic for my taste. Now something in a damp marsh..." The Blue Bear gave a final push, and the two entered the throne room.

In the center of the throne room sat a great lavender bear on an elaborate wooden throne, which appeared to be carved from the living trunk of the tree. The room was flooded with golden light from a high leafy dome, and paintings of bears engaging in all sorts of activities covered the walls. A large bookcase sat at one side of the room, filled with stories and tales concerning bears, and a mossy carpet covered the floor. Next to the throne was a small wooden chair, where the Little Pink Bear sat. He seemed unusually stiff compared to the other bears Seymour had seen in the clearing, and didn't move at all.

As the odd pair approached the throne, the Lavender Bear closed the picture book he had been reading. Speaking in a merry growl he asked, "Well Corporal Moody, what seems to be the problem? And who is your little feathered friend?"

The duck was relieved to hear the King speak so pleasantly, and relaxed his wings a bit.

"Perhaps this won't be as bad as I thought," he mused. "After all, he does seem smarter than the average bear."

Standing before the King, Corporal Moody gave a low bow, in which his nose touched the floor. After a smart salute he declared, "Your Majesty, we have caught this wise-quacking duck in our clearing. He seems to have eluded our sentry, and just now created great excitement among the bears. We are certain he is a spy sent by the squirrels."

The Lavender Bear removed his tin crown, which was set with pale purple diamonds and amethysts, and scratched his head doubtfully. "Well that certainly sounds serious, but he doesn't appear fowl-tempered. What does the prisoner have to say for himself?"

The Blue Bear shoved Seymour forward a step and hissed, "Bow!" The duck waddled up to the throne and did his best to bow, with undignified results.

Picking himself up, he faced the King. "Your most plushlike Majesty, I am innocent of all charges! I don't know any squirrels, and I only landed in your clearing because I was tired. I am a homeless traveler, who has seen many strange lands, but I will admit this is the strangest!"

16

"You seem to have made quite an impact on our clearing," mused the King, frowning slightly.

With a worried look, Seymour pleaded, "I don't think I even made a dent. All I know is I didn't bear right and I didn't bear left, so I seem to have come to Bear Center!"

"We'll see what my advisor has to say on the matter," decided the King. Picking up the Little Pink Bear from its chair, the Lavender Bear lovingly wound a golden key that stuck out of the fur on the little bear's back. Sitting the bear in its chair once again, the King asked, "Can this duck be trusted, or is he our enemy?"

The Little Pink Bear saluted stiffly, and replied in a slightly wheezy voice, "Hurrah for the King of Bear Center! The duck is an innocent traveler. He will do no harm." With that, the Pink Bear became as lifeless as before.

"There now!" chuckled the Lavender Bear. "All that fuss over nothing. The Pink Bear always tells the truth." With great pride in his voice he continued, "The Pink Bear is a tremendous help in ruling my kingdom. I do hope you will stay for a visit and allow us to make up for our unfriendly welcome. We really are a pleasant little country."

With a glance at the Blue Bear, who seemed suitably ashamed, Seymour replied good-naturedly, "I'd be delighted! Perhaps Corporal Moody would show me the rest of your city." This cheered the Blue Bear, who had been feeling a bit foolish.

"You have a marvelous palace here," the duck continued as he waddled around the throne room. He stopped by a small table sitting in front of a large open window which overlooked the town. On the tabletop sat a good-sized golden cube. With a hop and a flap of his wings, Seymour alighted on top of the cube to glance through the window for a better view of the clearing. Suddenly he was shot through the air and out the window, as the cube seemed to explode beneath him.

"Look out!" he screeched in a flurry of feathers, "It's an eruption!"

The King and the Blue Bear seemed undisturbed, and merely watched with curiosity as Seymour struggled to regain control of his movements. With a quick flap and flutter of wings, he flew back into the throne room. "What was that?" he asked, once his breath had returned.

"That's my BEBO," replied the King with pride in his voice. "It's the only one in the world."

Seymour walked back to the golden cube for a closer look. To his surprise, the top was now open, and a golden bear was sticking out of the cube. It

wobbled back and forth, as if it were on a spring. On each side of the cube ran the letters B, E, B, O. "Why, it's just a jack-in-the-box," he chuckled.

The King looked very offended. "No it isn't. It's a BEar-in-the-BOx. That's where it gets its name. BEBO."

"What does it do, besides assault visitors?" the duck asked skeptically.

The King looked a bit uncomfortable at this, and rubbed his nose with his paw. "It was a gift from Princess Ozma, the beautiful princess who rules all of Oz from her castle in the Emerald City," he replied nonchalantly. "It was a thank-you for my valuable help in rescuing her when she was kidnapped by Ugu the Shoemaker. She said I would find it most useful and amusing."

"But what does it do?" pressed Seymour, looking distinctly unimpressed.

"Well...we don't really know," admitted the King in an agony of embarrassment. "But it's bound to come in handy sometime. Ozma said so."

"I see," said Seymour rather flatly. "You'll have to excuse me for not being more enthusiastic, but I don't like having my tail feathers ruffled."

At this awkward moment there came a gentle cough from the entrance to the throne room.

The Lavender Bear

"Corporal Honey reporting for sentry duty!" stated the large Yellow Bear who was standing in the doorway.

"Ah, yes, Corporal," greeted the King with a salute, glad of the interruption. "Nothing has been reported, aside from the arrival of our feathered friend here. I think you'll have an uneventful shift." As the Yellow Bear turned to leave, the King turned to Seymour.

"Evening is upon us. Why don't you spend the night here in my treetop home? It really would be pleasant to have the company. In the morning when you are rested, Corporal Moody will return and we can give you a proper tour of Bear Center."

"That would be lovely," replied the tired duck, who had been discreetly yawning behind his wing. "I have had a full day."

While the Blue Bear chatted and planned the morning's tour with the King, Seymour found himself a soft cushion to nest in and, tucking his beak under his right wing, was soon quietly sleeping.

Babies Afloat

Carried by a strong wind, the pink cloud of babies sped through the sky, swiftly outdistancing the fastest of the storks who pursued them. In no time at all there was nothing to be seen below but desert in all directions. The baby rebels celebrated their freedom by cavorting in the billowy cloud cushions and raiding the milk cupboard and the biscuit box. Soon, exhausted from the day's excitement, they slept soundly as night drew near.

In the morning, the babies found their situation was not much different, and some began to doubt the wisdom of releasing all their sheep guardians. There was still plenty of milk left to nourish the hungry babies, along with many clean baby-bottles, and piles of fresh diapers. However, the babies had never had to fend for themselves, having been waited on all their lives, and didn't know how to go about performing the simplest tasks. Consequently, they began to fuss and become cranky. Missing their scheduled naps did nothing to improve the mood of the crew on the runaway cloud.

Feeling quite pleased with himself for cleverly executing his plan, the King of the babies was steadily gazing at the ground through his spyglass, looking about to see if he could find what he was looking for. Finally a change of scenery could be seen. The desert was ending and a new, blue land could be viewed below. This distracted the babies, who had no idea where they were heading, but approved of the change of view.

As evening arrived, the King was still watching the ground, which had turned yellow, when suddenly he became quite excited. With several gurgles of pleasure, he grabbed the remains of the tethers which had held the pink cloud above Merryland. Throwing them over the side of the cloud the tethers tangled in the branches of the treetops below, bringing the cloud to an abrupt stop. The other babies, not expecting such a sudden halt to their journey, were thrown against the soft pillows and at once began to cry and wail. Only the discovery of the jelly cupboard, which had opened and spilled its sweet contents with the jarring stop, eventually quieted them.

Ignoring the deafening commotion, the King bounced to the edge of the cloud and looked more intently at the ground below. Bouncing and spinning with joy, the King threw his spyglass aside and managed to insert both his feet into his mouth. He knew that true happiness was close at hand for on the ground below he had found what he was looking for!

*   *   *   *   *

"What a beautiful evening this has been," thought the Yellow Bear as he stood at the edge of the forest. His shift at the sentry post of Bear Center was almost over and soon the little Brown Bear would come to relieve him. In fact, there was little to relieve him from, for he loved to spend time alone in the forest at night, watching the stars. Nobody had ever successfully attacked Bear Center, but as the King had often warned, that didn't mean the bears could let down their guard.

As the Yellow Bear stood gazing at the sky above, he began to hum a quiet tune to himself,

Rum tum diddly dum
dum tum tiddly dee,

*A sentry bear must bear the best
responsibility.
For though the foe
may creep and lurk
in bushes near a tree,
The sentry gets to stay up late
with stars for company.*

Just as he was finishing his verse, the Yellow Bear heard a rustling in the bushes under a large tree to his right.

"Halt! Who goes there?" he growled in his most threatening manner. The thicket at once became still, and again the clearing fell silent. The Yellow Bear rubbed his nose and peered into the darkness. All at once he heard a loud rusty squeaking from the bushes to his left. He turned just in time to see a large goldenberry bush rustle and become still. "Come out of there at once!" he ordered in a loud voice. The only answer that came from the bush was another squeaking noise.

"I'll bet it's those young cubs, the Lemon and Tangerine Bears. No respect for their elders. Come on out now, before I come in after you! As it is I'll have to report you to the King for being out after hours!"

Sticking his head into the midst of the goldenberry bush he squinted and peered through the leaves. Then, with a muffled squeak, the Yellow Bear disappeared head first and tail last into the goldenberry bush, and the forest was once again peaceful and silent.

*   *   *   *   *

The morning dew was fresh when the little Brown Bear rounded the corner of the forest path and stepped out of the trees to the sentry post. He immediately noticed that something was amiss. In fact, someone was amissing!

"Yooo-hoo!" he yodeled, looking all around the clearing. "I'm here to relieve you. You can come out now and go back to your tree." Silence was the only response. Looking about in the pearly light, the little Brown Bear lowered his popgun and searched the perimeter of the forest for signs of the Yellow Bear.

"How peculiar," thought the little Brown Bear, leaning on his little tin popgun. "This has never happened before. None of the bears would ever want to leave this lovely forest, especially in the middle of the night."

As he conducted a second careful search of the sentry area and the surrounding wilderness, the little Brown Bear discovered the Yellow Bear's bright tin trumpet, in a patch of gorse and goldenberry. Now thoroughly alarmed, he galloped back to Bear Center to warn the King and alert the remaining bears. Bear Center was in danger!

Strange Disappearances

The bright morning sun shone merrily into the palace rooms, rousing Seymour from a pleasant night's slumber. As he stretched and waddled about the throne room, he was once again fascinated by the golden box of the BEBO which rested on its low table by the window. Gently brushing the solid gold object with his wing, he mused to himself, "Hmm... very pretty... but not of any practical use that I can see... I wonder how you trip the hinge?" Turning the box over to look at the underside, the lid suddenly opened and the golden bear once again flung itself from its confinement, hitting the duck's breast with such force that poor Seymour was knocked to the ground.

"Very sorry about that," blustered the Lavender Bear as he trotted into the room and hurried to the duck's aid. "I never have figured out how to open the BEBO—it just seems to jump out whenever it likes. To be honest, it usually frightens the stuffing out of me. I do hope that wasn't Ozma's intention when she presented it to me!"

Replacing the golden box on its table, the King invited the white duck to accompany him to the ground below and begin his tour of Bear Center. Seymour flew down from the castle, while the Lavender Bear climbed down the tree. Waiting below was the Blue Bear, who wore a large golden sash in honor of their visitor.

There were many bears going about their business, playing Who's-Got-the-Button, and Hide-and-Seek, but Seymour's attention was instantly drawn to three unusual bears that were corralled in the center of the clearing. These bears were made from olive green plush and stood on all fours, blankly staring straight ahead. The bears appeared lifeless and were not attired in fancy clothing like the other inhabitants of Bear Center, but held bits tightly in their mouths to which reins were attached. Each bear was mounted to a small wheeled platform.

"Ah, the transportation is ready," the King growled happily. "You'll be seeing Bear Center in style!" The Lavender Bear and Blue Bear each mounted one of the wheeled bears, and motioned for Seymour to do the same.

"I never expected to take up bear-back riding," the duck grumbled under his breath, as he flew to the back of the third bear. Here he settled comfortably on the plushy beast and waited.

The King and Corporal Moody began to move, but to Seymour's surprise they didn't ride the bears. Instead they propelled themselves by pushing their feet against the ground, pulling the wheeled bears along beneath them. Indeed, the wheeled bears seemed unable to move at all on their own, and only gave the viewer the impression of being ridden.

"Well, if that isn't the silliest thing I've ever seen!" cried the duck. The bears stopped and looked back at Seymour, realizing that he hadn't moved along with them. "What's the matter?" asked the Blue Bear, "haven't you ever ridden before?"

"As a matter of fact, I haven't. But you aren't riding—you're just sitting and dragging that silly bear along between your legs!"

"Well, of course — how else do you ride?"

While Seymour spluttered, trying to think of an answer, the two bears held a quick consultation.

Realizing that the duck's feet would never reach the ground, each bear took a rein and towed Seymour's wheeled bear along behind them. "Riding is such good exercise," commented the King as he trotted along. "I'm always much more tired after a ride than after a walk."

"I'm not surprised," muttered Seymour.

Bear Center was a good sized clearing which Seymour had already seen rather thoroughly the previous day. However, beyond the trees were the button bushes and fields of plush as well as other supplies that provided the means of creating new residents. The various materials were gathered on a regular basis, and taken to the tree of the Threadbears. These Threadbears were very important residents of Bear Center—they were responsible for keeping the population in tip-top shape. If a bear ever tore itself on a bramblebush, or lost an eye through carelessness, he only needed to find his way to the Threadbears, who pulled strands from their own multi-colored bodies to make the necessary repairs in practically no time at all. As they were kept very busy by such an active population, the Threadbears did not emerge from their tree very often. In general, they found the games and noise of the Bear Center

residents too distracting, so they kept to themselves. Seymour made appropriate clucking sounds as Corporal Moody explained all of this to him, and soon the trio moved past the Threadbears and toward a great field.

"On your left," intoned the Blue Bear in his best guide voice, "you can see the source of our many colors of fine plush." Indeed, the ground had the appearance of a patchwork quilt, with almost every imaginable color present! The effect was like that of moss under trees, but far more brilliant.

"Isn't that something," quacked Seymour, amazed in spite of himself. "I've never seen so much color in one spot—but isn't something missing?" Casting a bright eye on the King, he realized what was lacking. "Where is the lavender plush that you were created from, your Majesty?" The Lavender Bear seemed to have a pink glow of embarrassment about him, and the Blue Bear quickly scooted Seymour further forward.

"It's considered rude to discuss the king's plush," he whispered noisily in the duck's ear. "You see, our ruler was formed from a patch of royal purple that grew in the very center of the plush fields. It was the only spot of purple in the entire area. Unfortunately, he was caught in a rainstorm shortly afterward, and has never been the same since."

"Wasn't his color fast?" asked the duck sympathetically.

"Fast? Why it ran right out of him! We're lucky he remained lavender." Pausing to adjust his sash, which had slipped from his shoulder, the bear continued. "Oddly enough, the purple plush was uprooted and has never grown again."

When the King caught up to them, Seymour and the Blue Bear were busy discussing the yield from the various pin cushion flowers at their feet. Soon, they were all talking merrily and making their way back down the path that led to the central clearing.

Upon re-entering the clearing, the Lavender Bear was distressed to find all his subjects hopping about in an agitated fashion calling for him. Spotting the lavender ruler, the little Brown Bear rushed forward and ran in frantic circles around the King piping, "He's gone! Nowhere to be found! Completely vanished!"

Unable to make sense of the commotion or to stop the Brown Bear, the King calmly extended his silver scepter and tripped the small bear who skidded to a halt at his feet. Leaning forward and towering over the little Brown Bear, the King smiled reassuringly and in a calm voice asked him to start his tale at the beginning.

"Corporal Waddle reporting, sir!" the Brown Bear stated with a salute while continuing to lay on the ground below the King. "I was going to relieve Corporal Honey at the sentry post — and he wasn't there," gasped the little bear. "All I could find was his tin trumpet, which was laying in the grass near a large goldenberry bush." Handing the party favor to the King, the Brown Bear sat up in the grass while the other bears crowded closer to the King to examine the evidence.

"It's most unlike Corporal Honey to wander off and leave his noise-maker behind," pondered the fuzzy monarch. "Perhaps we should all go to the sentry post and have a good look-see."

With that, the entire assembly trotted off to the sentry area, where everything remained peaceful and quiet. After making a thorough search of the area, the King began issuing orders to the other bears.

"Split up into pairs and comb the woods for Corporal Honey. Don't lose sight of your partner, and be sure to watch out for squirrels. I shall return to the palace with Corporal Moody and

36

consult the Pink Bear to see if he has any solution to this puzzle. Everyone should meet back at Bear Center in two hours time and give their reports."

Spinning on his heel, the Lavender Bear started down the path, followed by the Blue Bear and Seymour. Corporal Waddle wasted no time in dividing up the bears and sending them out into the woods. Soon, the clearing stood empty except for the little Brown Bear, who resumed sentry duty.

A quarter of an hour quietly passed before the little Brown Bear heard a squeaking sound coming from a thicket of goldenrod. Moving closer to see if some of the bears had returned to register a report, Corporal Waddle called out in the direction of the noise but was not answered. Parting the tall goldenrod to get a better look, the little Brown Bear let out a gasp of surprise and was promptly swallowed into the thicket. After a moment or two, a large black baby pram slowly rose out of the thicket and into the sky, being pulled into the air by a heavy braid of pink woolen yarn. Inside its closed hood, the little Brown Bear blew his emergency whistle and tried to free himself, but his cries and noises were barely audible and too muffled to be heard on the ground below.

Barely Any Bears

Back in his throne room, the King paced the floor while the Blue Bear vented his anger. "Those rotten squirrels have really done it this time!" he exclaimed. "And after we had all that trouble last fall. I thought we were rid of them for good."

"What exactly is the problem with the squirrels?" asked Seymour in amusement. "I haven't seen a single squirrel since my arrival."

The King heaved a sigh, and threw himself onto his throne. Pushing his crown back from his forehead, he put his feet up and replied, "The squirrels live in the next forest up the river from us. They have a perfectly good forest of their own, but for some reason the Squirrel King has always envied us."

"They want our homes!" exclaimed the Blue Bear indignantly. "They say our hollow trees would make perfect storage vaults for their nasty little nuts." He flopped down on the floor and began shredding leaves, while the King continued the story.

"Last autumn the Squirrel King and his subjects floated down the river in their walnut boats, and tried to attack Bear Center. They pelted us with spoiled nuts, but of course that had no ill effect on my subjects. It was quite a mess to clean up later," he continued thoughtfully. "We managed to drive them away from our land. But since then, our sentries have been on double alert in case of a repeat attack."

"The King of the Squirrels is just plain greedy, and that's never a nice quality. Especially in a king," added the Blue Bear.

Seymour, hoping to give the maligned ruler the benefit of the doubt, hopped onto a stool next to the King's chair and asked, "Are you certain that the squirrels are behind all this? There could be another perfectly innocent explanation for the missing Yellow Bear. Isn't there some way to check?"

The King straightened in his throne and smiled at the white duck, "Let's see what the Pink Bear has to say on the matter!" Reaching to his side, the King lifted the Pink Bear from his chair and turned the key in his back. Addressing the stuffed advisor, the King asked, "Where has Corporal Honey gone?"

"The Corporal is with the babies," was the reply.

"Babies? There are no babies in Bear Center! You must be mistaken. Are you sure that he hasn't been abducted by the squirrels?"

"The Corporal is with the babies," the Pink Bear replied firmly.

The three inhabitants of the throne room looked at each other in confusion. "Babies have never been permitted near Bear Center," the Blue Bear explained to Seymour. "We're afraid our constitutions couldn't stand the strain."

"Oh, but there's nothing cuter than a baby chewing the ears off its first teddy bear," replied Seymour. "The little tykes are just adorable!"

The two bears glared at the duck coldly. "Are you quite mad?" the King asked.

"Well, I have some cousins who are loons, and my uncle's a bit daffy," Seymour answered cheerfully. "But I've always had a clear head."

The Blue Bear groaned, and explained, "You have to see this from our point of view. It may be adorable, but how would you feel being served up to someone with dressing and sauce for dinner?

Being given to a child is the worst punishment a bear knows."

"I hadn't thought of it in quite that way," Seymour said thoughtfully. "But it may not be as bad as you think. After all, there's a great deal of love involved."

The bears did not look convinced. "I think I'll try a different approach and see what we get," the King said, turning his attention back to his advisor. "The Pink Bear always tells the truth, but his answers don't always make perfect sense." Re-winding the Pink Bear, the King asked, "How are my subjects getting along with their search?"

"You only have four subjects left searching," replied the Pink Bear after a moments pause.

"Four!" cried the King. "There are a great many more than four bears searching the woods!"

"Now you're at two," corrected the Pink Bear flatly.

The King stood on his throne, pulling at his ears in distress. "How can there be only two bears left? What happened to the others?"

"They are all with the babies," the Pink Bear answered, after which he would say no more.

"This is unbearable!" stormed the King, who leapt from the throne shaking his scepter. The

King's scepter was very special indeed. If the King waved his scepter in a circle three times, and asked to be shown anything in all the land of Oz, the image of that item would appear before him. Swiftly rotating the scepter, the Lavender Bear commanded in a loud growl, "Show me Corporal Honey."

A pink mist seemed to rise from the floor, and suddenly an image of Corporal Honey appeared, locked in the embrace of a chubby baby. The Yellow Bear's left ear looked a bit ragged, and his right arm seemed to hang limp at his side.

"Oh, the savages!" shuddered the Blue Bear, turning away. "This is too painful to watch."

"Oh, I don't know," the sharp-eyed duck replied. "He certainly does look happy." Oddly enough, the Yellow Bear did look pleased and relaxed, despite the damage he had suffered.

As the image began to fade away, the Blue Bear turned to the troubled King. "The Pink Bear does seem to know what's what, but we still don't know where everyone is! How could these monstrous babies outwit such clever bears?"

Waving the scepter again, the King commanded, "Show me where the babies are hiding." The pink mist rose from the floor again,

but this time nothing else appeared. The King shook his scepter a few times and tapped it on the floor looking puzzled.

"That's odd. This doesn't appear to be a place I'm familiar with in the forest." There was some variation to the pink area that hovered in front of the King, but the image remained decidedly pink and soon began to fade.

"I've seen enough!" muttered the King. "This is more than I can bear. I'll simply have to go get help." Hurrying to a closet, the King pulled out a shiny tin pogo stick. "I'm going to make a dash for the castle of the Tin Woodman. Perhaps he can help me regain my subjects."

Climbing from the treehouse with the pogo stick in tow, the King shouted back to the Blue Bear and Seymour. "Stay indoors and guard the castle! Don't be foolish and go out wandering or get captured. I'll return as swiftly as I can!"

With a mighty bound the Lavender Bear leaped upon his pogo stick and swiftly bounced out of sight.

The Squirrel King

Not very far from Bear Center (as the duck flies) was the kingdom of the squirrels. Their forest consisted mainly of golden oak trees which provided piles of lovely amber colored acorns that the squirrels systematically gathered, sorted and stored. The many inhabitants of this grove were diligent workers who rarely entertained visitors and who were generally suspicious of outsiders. The ruler of this area of forest was a large single-minded grey squirrel with red feet and a bright red tail who encouraged his subjects to work long hours and take as few breaks from their toils as possible. Even so, the squirrels didn't mind the work, for the acorns they gathered were their main source of food. At other times of the year, the squirrels busied themselves by tending their hoard of nuts and by constructing walnut-shell boats.

From his vantage point high atop a tall oak tree, the King of the Squirrels chattered orders to his many subjects who were running round the large tree trunks gathering acorns. A large brown squirrel ran up the branch closest to the King to give a progress report.

"We are running out of storage space for the nuts we have harvested, Your Majesty," he stated with a bowed head.

"What!" snapped the King, who looked at the squirrel disapprovingly. "We can't be out of storage already. We haven't even started to gather nuts from Grove 7 yet."

"All the same Your Highness, the storage trees are filling up rapidly, and I don't think that we will even need to start work on that area. The crops have been so abundant this year that we already have more than enough nuts stored to last us until next season. Shall I tell the workers that they can stop once the storage trees are full? It will be nice to get an early start on the counting and sorting."

The Squirrel King tottered in a circle as if he would faint. "STOP EARLY !?! Nobody will stop gathering early! If the storage areas are filled, we will just have to create *more* storage areas," he cried, with an envious glance in the direction of Bear Center. Running back and forth on his branch, the King worked himself into a frenzy, his red tail twitching in spasms. "Tell everyone to work faster and gather every single acorn in the forest! Once the storage trees are filled, they can pile the surplus acorns in the area below this tree. If anyone complains, remind them that this will only mean more acorn pies and nut breads for all of us."

Dismissing the brown squirrel with a wave, the King once again was alone in his tree. Running to the very topmost branch, the crabby ruler maneuvered to get a better view of Bear Center. "If only those nasty bears hadn't driven us out of their clearing! Why, with their trees and mine combined, I could store twice as many acorns as I can now. What do bears want with trees anyway?"

Gazing in the direction of the bear's clearing, the Squirrel King rubbed his eyes and peered intently. There above the yellow laburnums was a large pink cloud which seemed to hover over the trees without moving, in spite of a stiff breeze blowing through the branches.

"Now what in the name of Ozma is that doing there?" he muttered to himself as he turned and scampered down to his nest in the branches below.

Once inside his leafy nest, the King quickly located his Magic Orb. This was an unusual black ball, made of some unknown material. When the King asked a question and shook the Orb, words were slowly revealed, floating in a dark liquid just under a small window at the bottom of the ball. The King could then read the message that appeared in answer to his question. No one knew where the orb had come from, but the King found it to be very useful. He generally used this device to predict rain storms so he could protect his nut hoards from rotting, but now he had a different question to ask.

"What is the pink cloud above Bear Center?" he asked, shaking the Orb.

The letters slowly began to get clearer as they floated to the window, spelling out the answer:

"PLEASE TRY AGAIN."

The King shook the orb impatiently, "Has something happened to the bears of Bear Center?"

"MY SOURCES SAY YES."

The Squirrel King danced in circles with glee, shaking the Orb again. "Has the King left Bear Center?"

"Yes, Definitely."

Quickly forming a plan, the King of the Squirrels tossed the Magic Orb aside. Jumping from his nest and scampering down the tree, he immediately began ordering his tired subjects to work faster. Once all the acorns had been gathered, the squirrels would load their walnut boats with the surplus and head downstream for Bear Center. This time their attack would be unchallenged!

Under Siege

In the midst of the pink cloud, high above Bear Center, peace and contentment reigned. Bears and babies were both happy and settled, cuddling together on the soft fleecy cloud cushions. The King of the Babies had claimed the large Yellow Bear as his own, and had given up his spyglass. He no longer needed to search the ground, for he had found what he was looking for.

Of course, the bears had not been immediately won over. When the Yellow Bear was first caught in the squeaky baby pram, he struggled to get free. Feeling himself being pulled through the air, he decided to wait and see what would happen next. After landing on the pink cloud, the top of the pram sprung open, and Corporal Honey found himself completely surrounded by babies. Many a weaker bear would have broken down in fear, but Corporal Honey sat stiffly in the pram, glaring at the little faces around him. Suddenly a chubby baby pushed its way through the crowd and, with a great leap, launched itself into the pram. Gurgling with pleasure, the baby hugged the Yellow Bear tightly, covering him with kisses. Lingering over the bear's left ear, the baby was soon contentedly sucking and gumming the ear, gurgling soft happy sounds. Corporal Honey found to his surprise that this was the most enjoyable thing that had ever happened to him, despite the resulting dampness. Relaxing, he allowed his baby captor to do as it pleased, deciding that he would be quite content in his predicament.

The other babies lost no time in sending all the prams down to the forest below. As the other bears began to arrive, the scene repeated itself time and again. Each bear was claimed by a baby, and to their surprise the bears found that babies were not the monsters they had been led to believe. In fact, the bears were completely happy in their captivity.

*　*　*　*　*

Seymour and the Blue Bear didn't know what to do. With the King gone, and the rest of the bears vanished, there seemed to be little they *could* do but wait.

Under Siege

"I don't like this at all," moaned the Blue Bear. "It's all very well for you, you can fly away any time you choose. I feel like a piece of bait just waiting for a big fat baby to clamp on to me."

As the Blue Bear fretted and paced the throne room, Seymour tried to console him, but met with little success. After carefully pushing the golden BEBO out of the way, he hopped up on the low table and took another long look through one of the throne room windows. He was struck with a thought.

"Where exactly is the King going for help?" he asked.

"He said he was headed to the palace of the Tin Woodman," replied the Blue Bear grumpily. "That's the ruler of this section of the land of Oz. We've never needed to call upon him before, but this is the greatest catastrophe we've ever encountered."

Seymour looked doubtful. "What exactly would he be able to do?" he wondered, as politely as possible for fear of further upsetting the Blue Bear.

"Well, he may not be able to do anything himself," Corporal Moody admitted thoughtfully, "But he is a close friend of Princess Ozma who has many magical powers at her command. I know she could do something to set those babies straight."

As he looked out the window again, Seymour gave a sudden start. "How long will it take for the King to return?" he asked, with a wobble in his voice.

"Oh, I don't know. A few days I suppose," returned the Blue Bear impatiently. "Why?"

"Well, don't look now but a fleet of walnut boats seems to be making its way down the river towards us," replied Seymour in a frightened quack. Corporal Moody somersaulted to the window in a panic, and saw that Seymour was right.

"I don't believe it!" he whimpered. "How could the squirrels have known we were defenseless? What can we do?" Sinking into a chair, the Blue Bear waved his feet in the air disconsolately and sucked on his paws. "If only there were more of us! We could call out the calvary and drive them back again."

"What calvary?" asked Seymour hopefully. "Do you mean there are still bears here that could help us?"

"Well, it's not really a calvary. They're our transport bears. You know the kind—we rode on them only this morning. When mounted by a herd

of fierce bears, the calvary can be quite intimidating."

"I really don't see what good they would do us now," said Seymour.

From below, the sound of chattering could be heard. The first squirrels had landed and were starting to run wild through Bear Center, checking out the hollow trees and searching for signs of any bears. As the squirrels leapt and scurried from branch to branch, Seymour shivered and wondered what the Blue Bear's fate might be. The white duck could escape at any time, but didn't feel that it would be fair to desert his new friend. "And besides, I'm not about to let a troupe of squirrels lord it over me!" he said to himself. So, as the hordes of invaders climbed nearer, the duck and the bear prepared themselves to meet the enemy.

56

The Tin Woodman Arrives

On the Winkie River, a curious boat floated swiftly toward Bear Center. It was formed from a great corn cob, with a red sail, and contained three passengers — a man made of tin, a man made of straw, and the King of the Bears.

"It's most kind of you to come back to Bear Center with me like this," said the Lavender Bear. "I can't imagine what I would have done if you hadn't been able to get away."

"Tut, tut. Think nothing of it," replied the metal ruler, cheerfully pulling on his oar. "And isn't it lucky that the Scarecrow happened to be visiting today!"

The Lavender Bear was indeed traveling in exalted company, for the Tin Woodman and the Scarecrow are quite possibly the most famous and beloved inhabitants in all of Oz.

At the back of the corncob boat, the man of straw was minding the rudder. "Don't you worry," he called to the Lavender Bear, "We'll find a way to reclaim your subjects!"

The Tin Woodman and the Scarecrow had been through numerous adventures and had found there were few problems they couldn't solve by working together. When the Lavender Bear had arrived at the palace of the Tin Woodman and explained the puzzle facing him, it seemed the easiest solution would be to revisit Bear Center and examine the situation first hand. The corncob boat was decided upon as the simplest method of transporting the three friends, especially as the King of Bear Center was uneasy at the thought of traveling by foot anywhere that a baby might snatch him.

"We should be nearing Bear Center after the next bend in the river," announced the Scarecrow, consulting a map.

The Lavender Bear looked about anxiously, almost afraid a baby might rear its head in the middle of the stream and pull him into the swirling waters. As the boat drew closer to Bear Center, he gave a start of surprise. "What are all these walnut boats doing here?" he cried. "The squirrels have attacked! And with no one to fight them off—I've lost my kingdom!"

The Tin Woodman Arrives

Indeed, if they hadn't known better, the three travelers might have thought they had landed in the kingdom of the squirrels. Everywhere they looked, squirrels scurried with armloads of nuts. The transport bears had been discovered and were being used to cart baskets of acorns, and the bears' hollows in the lovely laburnum trees were overflowing with nuts which spilled out onto the grass below.

"Nuts...*nuts!* Everywhere I look I see nuts!" wailed the Lavender Bear woefully.

"Don't be rude," murmured the Scarecrow to the distraught bear. "I'll grant you, they're acting a little crazed, but I wouldn't call them nuts."

The Tin Woodman rolled his eyes while the Lavender Bear sobbed and buried his snout in his paws. Giving the bear a hearty thump on the shoulder, the Tin Woodman reassured him, "Come now, all is not yet lost! I am still ruler of the Winkie Country and all of its inhabitants, so let's go have a word with these squirrels and see what happens. I'm sure they will be as polite and reasonable as any other inhabitant of Oz."

Stepping from the boat, the disheartened bear looked at the gleaming Winkie Emperor and muttered under his breath, "Polite and reasonable? I can tell you haven't had any squirrels at the palace recently."

Moving clumsily from the boat, the Scarecrow fluffed the straw in his chest and approached the first squirrel he met. Bowing in a courtly manner, he politely inquired if the squirrel in charge was anywhere nearby. His civilized request was met with chattering laughter as the squirrel hurled a spoiled acorn at him, barely missing his head. The little offender then ran back to the trees and resumed his hurried work.

"This may be more difficult than we expected," the Scarecrow said, turning to the Tin Woodman.

Seeing his friend treated so badly, the Tin Woodman strode boldly into the center of the clearing, where a great whirl of activity was taking place. Clearing his throat, and taking a majestic stance, he glared imperiously at the squirrels rushing through the trees. In his most regal voice he cried, "Stop this commotion at once and bring forth your leader!"

For a split second, all activity stopped and every squirrel stood motionless staring at the Tin Woodman. Then, as if on command, the squirrels suddenly began hurling nuts down upon the hapless man of tin. Being hit with acorns from all

sides at once resulted in a tremendous clattering against his metal. The noise was further heightened by the sound reverberating inside his hollow body. The din created so surprised and frightened the squirrels that they immediately scampered off into the woods chattering loudly, leaving the Tin Woodman alone in the center of the clearing. A small cheer rose from the tree of the Threadbears, who had been forgotten by the other bears during all the commotion and panic, but had been discovered and put to work by the squirrels, creating a new wardrobe for every one of the long-tailed invaders.

"Hooray for you!" shouted the Lavender Bear, who danced round in circles until he became dizzy and fell onto the grass.

The Tin Woodman took a moment to collect his thoughts which had been scrambled by the horrible noise within his head. The Scarecrow rushed to his side and began examining him for damage.

"You've sustained a few minor dents, but it looks like they will be easily put to rights once you get home." Looking at the Lavender Bear, who was lying woozily in the grass, the Scarecrow suppressed a giggle and said, "I don't think the squirrels will be thwarted for long, so we had better act quickly. Didn't you say that you left someone behind to keep an eye on things?"

Climbing to his feet, the Lavender Bear became serious and answered, "Yes indeed. Corporal Moody and Seymour the duck were left in charge and were told not to leave the throne room. Perhaps they are still there! Quickly, follow me!"

*   *   *   *   *

The King of the Squirrels was in the Lavender Bear's throne room madly rushing about in a state of extreme agitation, clutching the small Pink Bear. "Why won't this bear move or do as I command?" he ranted. Turning to Corporal Moody and baring his teeth, he threatened, "If you don't straighten up and start giving some answers pretty soon, I'll have you turned into blue cushions for my new throne! And I think I'll have them stuffed with white feathers!" This was said with an evil glance in Seymour's direction.

The Blue Bear had steadfastly refused to be of any assistance to the unwelcome intruder. "My name is Corporal Moody. I am in command of Bear Center while the Lavender Bear is away," was all he would say.

Seymour, on the other hand, had said plenty! When the squirrels landed in Bear Center, Seymour and the Blue Bear watched their progress through the kingdom and decided it was best to lay low in the hopes of not being discovered. They barricaded the entrance to the throne room and waited as quietly as possible in hopes that the squirrels would run through the area and continue on their way. The squirrels, of course, had no intention of leaving the grove and it was only a matter of time before they came upon the blocked entrance to the royal chambers. With the Squirrel King leading the assault, the animals quickly chewed their way through the walls into the Lavender Bear's quarters and confronted the pair of captives.

The Blue Bear and Seymour put up a tremendous fight, hurling anything that wasn't nailed down at their attackers. But with squirrels pouring into the room from every side, the pair were soon overpowered. Even then, Seymour flew in a rage at the King himself and squawked as loudly as possible while flapping his wings in the upstart ruler's face. It took four squirrels to subdue the enraged duck and as punishment, the King of the Squirrels ordered that Seymour's wings be clipped with a large wooden clothespin. At this treatment, the duck let forth a stream of violent language, threatening the King with all manner of bodily harm. The cruel squirrel simply laughed at his prisoner and ordered that his beak be clipped tightly shut as well. The poor white duck was left to sit in the corner, unable to move or speak.

The only two objects in the throne room that were not thrown at the attackers were the Pink Bear, who remained in his place at the side of the throne, and the BEBO, which remained by the window. With Corporal Moody securely bound in the corner next to the unfortunate white duck, the King of the Squirrels sent his minions to help unload acorns and relaxed a bit. Turning his attention to these two precious objects, the King relentlessly questioned the Blue Bear as to their use, but was given no information.

Just as the aggravated King was about to begin a fresh assault on the Blue Bear, the blocked entryway to the throne room reverberated with the sound of the Tin Woodman's gleaming axe. With two mighty blows, the entry was reopened, and a happy trio scrambled into the throne room to confront the usurper.

Under Observation

In her ruby palace in the south of the land of Oz, Glinda the good sorceress was having her morning cup of red hibiscus tea. Glinda, the beautiful ruler of the Quadling Country, is also a loyal subject of Princess Ozma, the ruler of all Oz. Between Glinda's sorcery and Ozma's fairy powers, as well as the Wizard of Oz's wizardry, the land of Oz is well protected from evildoers. Of course, it's difficult to keep track of everything happening in a land as large as Oz. This is why Glinda has her magical Book of Records. Everything happening anywhere in the world is recorded in this book, just as it happens. Every morning Glinda reads over the latest events in Oz, with an occasional glance at the happenings in the outside world. On this particular morning, Glinda was sharing the book with Princess Ozma herself, who had arrived the previous evening to visit and discuss affairs of state. While Glinda drank her tea, Ozma sipped on

Under Observation

a glass of pink limeade and scanned the events on the page before her.

"Now, here's something unusual," Ozma cried in surprise, setting down her glass (which was carved from a large diamond). "The King of the Squirrels has overtaken Bear Center. Now, what could have happened to all those nice bears?"

Glinda looked up in interest, and together the two rulers bent their lovely heads over the record book, scanning the previous pages for more information on the events in Bear Center. In this way they learned the entire story, from the disappearance of the bears, to the arrival of the squirrels.

"We must do something," Ozma declared, with an indignant expression in her pretty green eyes. "I won't have Bear Center destroyed by that nasty Squirrel King. I seem to recall having some problems with him in the past," she mused. "Perhaps I had better take a trip to the Winkie forest and see just what is going on."

"I don't think that will be necessary Princess," Glinda replied in her gentle voice, still scanning the book of records. "See here—the Tin Woodman and Scarecrow have just arrived, together with the lavender King of the Bears. I think we can count on them to solve whatever problems might exist, and remember, Nick Chopper is the Emperor of all the Winkie inhabitants."

Knowing she could count on her trusty old friends, Ozma agreed. "But just the same, I think we had better keep a close eye on that area for a while. If those naughty squirrels get out of hand, they'll have to answer to me." Smiling, she handed her breakfast plate to Glinda. "Now would you be a dear and pass me another of those delicious raspberry scones?"

* * * * *

Upon seeing the Lavender Bear entering his throne room, the Squirrel King instantly became defensive, his red tail bushing out to twice its usual size. "Get out at once! How dare you disturb me in my chambers unannounced!"

"*Your chambers!*" roared the Lavender Bear, and turning to the Tin Woodman, began to plead. "Don't let this imposter steal my kingdom from me! First my loyal subjects are bear-napped by babies, and now I'm overrun by squirrels. Where

68

will I go? What will I do?" Plopping down on the floor among the heaps of acorns brought in by the industrious squirrels, the distraught ruler buried his snout in his paws and groaned.

The Scarecrow and Tin Woodman barely noticed the Lavender Bear, for they were shocked to see the Blue Bear and the white duck trussed up in the corner.

"Now just what has been going on here?" asked the Tin Woodman in a cold voice. Fixing a gleaming eye on the Squirrel King, he began to twirl his axe threateningly. "What do you mean by mistreating those poor creatures and taking over this city? I seem to recall having trouble with you about a year ago — you tried to evict a village of rabbits! Something about their underground chambers being a perfect place to store nuts." Wiping a bit of acorn from his chest, the Tin Woodman shook his head in pity. "You silly creature! Surely you realize there's no need to store surplus nuts? Trees in Oz provide nuts year-round!"

"I don't care!" the Squirrel King retorted, stamping his little red feet. "It always pays to be prepared. I'm not going to be caught empty handed some day just because I didn't plan ahead! These trees had been deserted—well, practically. I'm simply putting them to good use." With this he plopped himself down on the Lavender Bear's throne.

The Scarecrow shook his head and tut-tutted at such audacious language. "Don't you know your subjects have all fled? You are the only squirrel left in Bear Center, and as the Tin Woodman is ruler even over you, I think you had better keep a civil tongue in your head. Now why don't you just go home?"

Infuriated, the squirrel jumped from the throne and raced around the room, chattering wildly. "Phooey on you! I won't go home! I hereby name this area Squirrel Center, and no other creatures are permitted in my domain!" Hopping up on the BEBO, which still sat on its little table, he glanced hopefully through the throne room window. "My squirrels haven't deserted me—they must still be out there. I'll call them all and have you put out! You can't order me around, I'll..." Without a warning, the golden BEBO sprang open, throwing the irate squirrel through the window, and down to the ground where he landed in a cartload of spoiled nuts.

"Ozma was right!" cheered the Lavender Bear gleefully. "The BEBO *has* come in handy!"

Hearing the hearty laughter of his enemies in the throne room, the humiliated squirrel climbed out of the nut cart and raced home to his own kingdom, where he stayed for a very long time.

Find the Babies

As soon as the intruding squirrel was dispatched, the Tin Woodman hurried to the aid of the hapless prisoners. Unpinning Seymour's beak and freeing his wings, the grateful duck flapped about the room gleefully.

"Thank you so much for rescuing us! Why, that nasty red rodent threatened to pluck me and use my feathers for stuffing. And that would have been nothing compared to the fate he had in store for the Blue Bear, who I might add, showed extreme bravery in the face of such adversity."

Corporal Moody, who would have blushed had his plush allowed it, had grabbed a broom and was busy sweeping nuts through the openings the squirrels had chewed through the walls and floor of the throne room.

"Thank you for your kind words," stated the Blue Bear humbly. "But I must admit that His Royal Nastiness was making me quite angry. If I had been able to get loose and clobber him, I'd have given it my best shot!"

The Lavender Bear made a mental note to remember to decorate the corporal for his bravery, but his thoughts quickly returned to his other problems. Wading across the room through piles of discarded nuts, the King picked up the Pink Bear from the floor and reinstated him on his little chair by the throne.

"Now gather round, and we'll try this again," he called to his friends. Winding the key that protruded from the Pink Bear, the anxious ruler asked, "Where are the bears who disappeared from Bear Center?"

The Pink Bear remained motionless for a few seconds and then answered, "The bears are with the babies."

"See! What did I tell you? We'll never find my poor subjects. They're stuck with those awful babies, and we can't get any clues as to where they are."

The Scarecrow had been observing the display quietly, letting his excellent brains turn the problem over. With a chuckle he said, "Why don't you wind him up again—only this time don't ask him where the bears are, ask him where the *babies* are!"

Find the Babies

The Lavender Bear let out a shout of glee, and did as he was instructed. After another moment of silence, the Pink Bear answered, "The babies are on the pink cloud."

No one present knew anything about a pink cloud. The Tin Woodman thought the cloud must be in the southern country of the Quadlings, where red was the favorite color, but the Scarecrow disagreed. After trying in vain to catch a glimpse of the sky through the dense laburnum branches, he asked Seymour to fly up and see if he could spot anything unusual. Seymour was happy to be of service and glad to stretch his wings, which were rather kinked from the clothespin. After only five minutes time, the white duck flew back into the throne room.

"I found it! If it were a giant, it couldn't be plainer. All we have to do is go down to the clearing and look up. The pink cloud is hovering directly over Bear Center!"

The assembly couldn't get out of the throne room fast enough. Seymour flew out of the window and down to the ground, while the Lavender Bear and Corporal Moody scrambled halfway down the tree and jumped the rest of the way. Only the Scarecrow and the Tin Woodman were careful in their descent, trying to maintain a bit of dignity. When the entire party had assembled in the clearing, they all looked up through the branches to see that there was indeed a large pink cloud hovering in the blue sky directly over Bear Center.

The Tin Woodman took charge and asked Seymour to fly closer to the cloud and see whether the bears of Bear Center were truly being held captive. He and the Scarecrow then tried to figure out why the cloud was stationary over the area when a stiff wind from the east was blowing. They were unable to think of a logical reason.

After several circles in the air, Seymour returned to the yellow ground and breathlessly gave his report. "I'm sorry to say I couldn't quite see over the edge of the cloud, but I did hear some noises that I can only describe as babylike. However, I did see something else. The cloud appears to be tethered to that large laburnum tree at the north end of the clearing."

"That's my house!" exclaimed Corporal Moody. "What do those babies mean by fastening themselves to my roof?"

The Lavender Bear moved closer to the tree in question and stated, "How very curious...the cloud seems to be held in place by almost invisible

strings of some sort. Look...if you squint in the sunlight you can just make them out. But how will we ever reach my bears? They must be desperate to return home by now, and I know they will expect me to save them. I can't see how we'll get to the cloud to free them. This is a difficult puzzle!"

While the King fretted, the Scarecrow and Tin Woodman smiled at each other. "You see, your Highness," the Scarecrow said, "if the cloud is attached to the treetop, and the treetop is attached to the tree trunk, then all we need to do is cut down the tree and topple the cloud to the ground."

This solution was met with cheers by all present except the Blue Bear, who would lose his home in the process. After giving it some thought however, he agreed to sacrifice his comfortable home to restore the populace of Bear Center. The promise of a room of his own in the palace helped to soften the blow. The Tin Woodman then took his gleaming ax and set to work felling the majestic tree. While he chopped, the King of the Bears paced anxiously in circles, eager to see his missing subjects. The Blue Bear busied himself making plans for his new home, and Seymour absentmindedly chewed on some stray wisps of straw from the Scarecrow's boot. With a final sharp chop at the base of the old tree, the Tin Woodman gave a warning shout. The tree tottered and a great clattering arose, as all the acorns stored within the trunk by the industrious squirrels tumbled to the earth below. The laburnum slowly toppled and fell with a thundering crash to a smooth landing in the center of the clearing, and as expected, the pink cloud descended with the tree, completely covering the glade.

Babies, Babies, Everywhere

The first thing Seymour noticed was the strange pink color that seemed to have coated everything in sight. Then, like the din of a warning siren, an unearthly wail rose all around as the babies recovered from the shock of being pulled from the sky. The noise was deafening, and, uncertain of what to do, the white duck flew to the branches of the nearest tree. From this vantage point, Seymour had an excellent view of the confusion on the ground.

When the pink cloud was pulled from the sky, the jolt caused the babies to become separated from their bears. Now the ground was covered with wailing babies. Of course, the infant making the loudest racket was the King of the Babies, who was turning quite purple in the face.

Meanwhile, the bears who had been knocked to the ground were frantically trying to return to their beloved little captors. As they raced about madly, the Lavender Bear stood in the midst of the mess pleading with his subjects to run for their lives. Instead, each bear continued looking until it found its baby. As each of the renegades regained the bear it had lost, the baby would become docile. Soon, all the crying had stopped and relative peace filled the forest.

The Lavender Bear stood in the clearing, aghast that his once loyal subjects were all willingly in the clutches of the babies. Only Corporal Moody remained at the King's side, using a toy drumstick to fend off any baby that crawled in their direction.

"Whatever shall we do?" the Blue Bear asked the King frantically. "All the bears seem to have had their brains rattled into thinking they are safe. Just look at what those ferocious creatures are doing to our friends! They're killing them with kindness! See how the poor chartreuse bear has lost an ear, and look over there at the Teal Bear — that poor fellow doesn't have a right arm!"

It was quite true that all of the bears were much the worse for wear, however none of them really minded because they were being loved so strongly by the babies. In fact, once a bear had been reunited with its particular baby, the bear would become motionless and gladly allow the baby to do all manner of unusual things. The kingdom of the Lavender Bear was in an uproar, and it appeared to be up to the Tin Woodman to sort out the whole mess.

The gleaming man of metal walked up to the largest baby he could find, and politely asked the baby who he was, and what his purpose was in coming to the Land of Oz. The King of the Babies, for the Tin Woodman had unwittingly singled out the self appointed leader of the troop, lay on his back with the Yellow Bear in his grasp. Chewing on the bear's left foot, the King of the Babies made happy gurgling noises while looking up, fascinated by his reflection in the body of the Tin Woodman.

The Scarecrow moved closer to see if he could be of any assistance. The baby, seeing the large stuffed man of straw coming close, dropped the Yellow Bear and lunged to grab the Scarecrow, who sidestepped the greedy baby just in time.

"That was close!" said the Scarecrow. "I feel like a fly in a frog pond — get too close and *zap!* — they get you!"

The Tin Woodman regarded the cherubic infant that lay on the ground before him, and replied, "But just look how sweet and innocent they are. I don't think they really want to destroy anything, they just have a bit too much enthusiasm in showing affection. I wish we could communicate with them and find out where they belong."

As if in response to the Tin Woodman's statement, the sky darkened and a rushing of wings could be heard. A large flock of storks made a graceful landing in the midst of the pink cloud, and folded their wings. Looking a bit disoriented, the leader of the storks approached the Scarecrow.

"I believe we have met once before," she said politely. "I seem to recall rescuing you from the middle of a river many years ago. Tell me, are you the ruler of this odd country?"

With a start of recognition, the Scarecrow replied, "You're quite right! You rescued me on my very first trip to the Emerald City, when I had foolishly become stuck on a pole in the middle of the river. But I'm not the ruler of this country—the Tin Woodman standing next to me is."

Nodding modestly, the Tin Woodman replied, "Actually, the Lavender Bear is the ruler of this particular area, however I am Emperor of the entire Winkie country, which is where you are. How may I help you?"

"We've come to retrieve our babies," the stork explained simply.

"YOUR babies!" cried the Lavender Bear. The King rose with a start and ran wildly at the stork. "What do you mean by unleashing your babies on an unsuspecting population of gullible bears? My subjects have all been bear-napped and brain-washed by these creatures, causing me no end of trouble. It appears that I've lost my subjects for good," he finished, choking back a sob.

The stork apologized profusely, explaining how the babies had fled from their proper home, and escaped their protectors.

"I shouldn't think the little savages needed much protection," sniffed the Blue Bear. "Look what they've done to my friends!"

The Scarecrow had been sitting by himself for some time, pondering the situation. Now he sat up with a sunny smile. "I think I may have a solution to the problem," he said cheerily. Turning to the Lavender Bear he asked, "Your Majesty wouldn't want to deny your subjects any happiness, would you?"

"Of course not," the King replied gruffly. "The happiness of my bears is the most important thing I protect. But how can I if they are going to fly off

with these babies? I won't have any subjects and will be of no use to anyone."

"What if you were to have a new crop of subjects?" asked the Scarecrow. "Would that make you happy?" Seeing the Lavender Bear's confusion, he explained. "Why not let these bears return with their babies? They will keep each other happy, and your Threadbears can quickly make a new population for Bear Center. In fact, I think the population could turn over on a regular basis—I'm sure the storks wouldn't mind traveling to Oz to pick up new bears for new babies. They could also return the old ones for repairs when needed. Bear Center would be providing a great service to the storks and the great outside world. And you would still be a King!"

The Lavender Bear took five minutes to think over the Scarecrow's proposal and, after a hurried consultation with the Blue Bear, agreed.

"It's a splendid idea! Corporal Moody has agreed to stay on and become my Prime Minister, since he has no more interest than I in babies. He will be in charge of training new bears, and ensuring that our quality doesn't drop."

Everyone was pleased with this decision, particularly the babies who seemed to understand that they had won their bears for good. While the Tin Woodman, Scarecrow, and stork leader discussed how to return the pink cloud to its proper location, the Lavender Bear and Corporal Moody made the other bears line up and file through the tree of the Threadbears, who quickly repaired all the bears until they were as good as new.

"I can't have you leaving Bear Center in shreds," explained the King. "What would people think?" At first the babies were a bit uneasy at losing their bears, even for a moment, but the storks explained what was happening in their own special language and managed to prevent another full scale baby riot.

When the stork leader realized that the pink cloud was on the ground only because the tethers were tangled in the fallen laburnum tree, she immediately had a solution for returning the babies to their proper home. Once the bears had all been repaired and returned to their babies, the storks carefully pulled the tethers from the tree branches. As soon as the pink cloud was freed, its natural buoyancy returned, and the cloud floated into the sky, bearing all its occupants and surrounded by storks. Holding the tethers in their beaks, the storks quickly flapped their strong wings and began to tow the cloud back to Merryland where it belonged.

The Lavender Bear stood below and sadly waved goodbye to his subjects, then cheered up considerably as the first new bear wandered out from the Threadbear's tree. "I can always use my scepter to check up on my bears at any time," he said contentedly. "They know I wouldn't desert them. And I still have the Little Pink Bear!"

With this thought to comfort him, the Lavender Bear turned to thank the Tin Woodman and Scarecrow for their help. Suddenly there was a brilliant flash and tinkling of bells. Ozma and Glinda appeared before the bewildered bear.

"We just couldn't stay away any longer," Ozma gaily explained. "After reading along with all your trials in the Book of Records, Glinda and I felt we should come and congratulate you personally for your generous sacrifice."

"Well, it really seemed the only thing to do," blustered the King, embarrassed by the beautiful fairy's attention. "I mean, I couldn't bear the thought of disappointing all my subjects. And really, it was the Scarecrow's idea after all..." He turned away, blushing a lovely rose color.

Babies, Babies, Everywhere

"The Scarecrow's brains have certainly served him well on this occasion," Glinda commented. The straw man ducked his head modestly, while the stately sorceress gazed searchingly around the clearing. "But where are the Blue Bear and white duck? They are to be congratulated, too."

Seymour and Corporal Moody tiptoed out from behind a large rock. "We saw this strange flash," began the duck. "And our nerves really couldn't take another shock," finished the bear, shamefacedly.

Ozma giggled, while Glinda produced two lovely ruby pendants. "These are in recognition of your great bravery when faced by insurmountable squirrels," she declared. "And I have another pendant for your Highness in recognition of your kindness to babies!"

The Lavender Bear was so pleased with his decoration, that he puffed out his chest until a seam burst. The entire group laughed aloud at this mishap, and the King beat a hasty retreat to the Threadbears, who had him repaired in record time.

By now the clearing was starting to fill with new bears, and Corporal Moody hastened to begin his job of training the newcomers. The Scarecrow and Tin Woodman politely refused an offer by Ozma to return them to the Tin Woodman's castle by means of her magic belt. The two friends preferred a leisurely trip by corn cob boat along the river. "And," the Tin Woodman declared, "I wouldn't mind stopping to take a peek at the Squirrel King's forest, just to make sure he isn't up to any more mischief!" Ozma agreed wholeheartedly with this plan, and the two friends set off along the river once again.

Seymour watched his friends disperse, and sighed as he prepared to continue his own journey. Just then he felt a tap upon his shoulder, and turned to find Ozma gazing at him hopefully. "Surely you won't leave without visiting the Emerald City?" she inquired. "I'm sure you'll find plenty there to amuse you, and I know my friends would all love to meet such a valiant duck."

"Why, I'd be honored," stammered the duck.

"Would you prefer to fly there on your own, or be transported together with Glinda and I?" Ozma asked. After being assured that transporting was not painful in any way, Seymour decided to try traveling by magic.

"After all," he considered, "when in Oz do as the Ozites do. Besides, my wings are still a bit sore from that clothespin." After a final round of good-byes, and promises to the King and Corporal Moody that he would visit again, Ozma, Glinda and Seymour vanished to the Emerald City. There the white duck was made to feel completely at home, and may be visiting still.

*   *   *   *   *

In the country of Merryland, above the Valley of Babies, the pink cloud was floating peacefully. As before, the pink sheep looked after their tiny charges, who were happy and contented to be in their proper place again. The King of the Babies had soon reached the age of being sent to Merryland by blossom. The pink sheep happily dispatched their charge to the ground below, and from there he traveled to the outside world, together with his beloved Yellow Bear.

Of course now there was a new 'biggest' baby, but he was not of the same adventurous nature as the previous King. He could make his presence known throughout the entire cloud when he felt the need, but the bears were now the center of attention, and there was little likelihood of another revolt. The storks flew old bears back to

Bear Center for repairs and replenished the cloud with new bears as needed. Tranquility reigned supreme ever after.

The End

OZ
from
Emerald City Press™

Exciting Oz Stories
from a New Generation of Authors and Artists

How the Wizard Came to Oz
Written and Illustrated by
Donald Abbott

How the Wizard Saved Oz
Written and Illustrated by
Donald Abbott

The Magic Chest of Oz
Written and Illustrated by
Donald Abbott

The Speckled Rose of Oz
Written and Illustrated by
Donald Abbott

Father Goose in Oz
Written and Illustrated by
Donald Abbott

The Giant Garden of Oz
Written and Illustrated by
Eric Shanower

Masquerade in Oz
Written and Illustrated by
Bill Campbell and Irwin Terry

The Lavender Bear of Oz
Written and Illustrated by
Bill Campbell and Irwin Terry

Nome King's Shadow in Oz
by Gilbert M. Sprague
Illustrated by Donald Abbott

The Patchwork Bride of Oz
by Gilbert M. Sprague
Illustrated by Denis McFarling

The Glass Cat of Oz
by David Hulan
Illustrated by George O'Connor

Christmas in Oz
by Robin Hess
Illustrated by Andrew Hess

Queen Ann in Oz
by Karyl Carlson & Eric Gjovaag
Illustrated by B. Campbell and I. Terry

The Magic Dishpan of Oz
by Jeff Freedman
Illustrated by Denis McFarling

If you enjoy the Oz books and want to know more about Oz, you may be interested in **The Royal Club of Oz**. Devoted to America's favorite fairyland, it is a club for everyone who loves the Oz books. For free information, please send a first-class stamp to:

The Royal Club of Oz
P.O. Box 714
New York, New York 10011

Or call toll-free: (800) 207-6968

Classic Oz Tales
from
Books of Wonder®

The Sea Fairies
by L. Frank Baum
Illustrated by John R. Neill

Sky Island
by L. Frank Baum
Illustrated by John R. Neill

Royal Book of Oz
by Ruth Plumly Thompson
Illustrated by John R. Neill

Kabumpo in Oz
by Ruth Plumly Thompson
Illustrated by John R. Neill

Captain Salt in Oz
by Ruth Plumly Thompson
Illustrated by John R. Neill

Handy Mandy in Oz
by Ruth Plumly Thompson
Illustrated by John R. Neill

The Silver Princess in Oz
by Ruth Plumly Thompson
Illustrated by John R. Neill

Ozoplaning with the Wizard
by Ruth Plumly Thompson
Illustrated by John R. Neill

The Wonder City of Oz
Written and Illustrated by
John R. Neill

The Scalawagons of Oz
Written and Illustrated by
John R. Neill

Lucky Bucky in Oz
Written and Illustrated by
John R. Neill

The Runaway in Oz
by John R. Neill
Illustrated by Eric Shanower

The Magical Mimics in Oz
by Jack Snow
Illustrated by Frank Kramer

The Shaggy Man of Oz
by Jack Snow
Illustrated by Frank Kramer

Merry Go Round in Oz
by Eloise Jarvis McGraw and Lauren McGraw
Illustrated by Dick Martin

If you enjoy the Oz books and want to know more about Oz, you may be interested in **The Royal Club of Oz**. Devoted to America's favorite fairyland, it is a club for everyone who loves the Oz books. For free information, please send a first-class stamp to:

The Royal Club of Oz
P.O. Box 714
New York, New York 10011

Or call toll-free: (800) 207-6968